The Race

(Human that is)

by: Harold I.
(Oyvin DeScoyvin)
Hughes

iUniverse, Inc.
New York Bloomington

The Race
Human that is

iUniverse books may be ordered through booksellers or by contacting:

iUniverse
1663 Liberty Drive
Bloomington, IN 47403
www.iuniverse.com
1-800-Authors (1-800-288-4677)

ISBN: 978-1-4401-7861-0 (pbk)
ISBN: 978-1-4401-7889-4 (ebook)

Printed in the United States of America

iUniverse rev. date: 10/1/09

How stupid does the Human "Race" really want to remain?

(The <u>Love</u> of MONEY is the root of all evil)

When we refer to **American.** It should mean north, central, and south Americas. And any shade of skin tone that resides in any country on those continents. (We are all "americans" speaking a few different languages, RIGHT?). You have to ask the question. Why do people want to separate themselves by skin tone, language, religion, or into any other nonsensical unreasonable or "stupid" categories? I'm not really sure about the rest of the world. But in the United States, they call Jews a race. I always thought that was a religion. Mexicans call themselves a raza, or race. People refer to the black race, the Asian race, the Latin race, and the white race. Just a minute now, we are all in the human **race**. .... Are we not? That is all around the world, not just the Americas.

PREFACE

You know, I have never really wanted children. Now that I think about it, I am glad I have never had any. I wouldn't want to subject any little person to growing up in this world. They would have to deal with a lot of other children that have not had any kind of rearing. I mean, I have difficulty dealing with children of today. Those children would be peers to any little person I would have fathered and tried to raise. I mean people are so stupid they can't even raise their own children. Parents of today want pills to do that for them. They think if a child is too hyper, "OH, they need some sort of a drug." It doesn't occur to them that maybe the child could use a bit of discipline and love. No one gives their children any guidance these days, and then they teach them to call the authorities when you try to discipline them. In all actuality kids crave discipline, it shows them that you love them enough to teach them right from wrong. Discipline should never be physical abuse, no one is entitled to that. And no one should be condemned to it either. It's just that idiots can go to extremes in both ways. They can be too extreme in discipline, and then the other end of the scale. Total neglect of any discipline at all. I withstood a few spankings in my youth, even one from a principle in school. (By the way spanking should **not** be your first choice of disciplinary action). Now days if a parent can't get their child on a television show (and make a little money at it) and get Brat Camp or someone like that to raise their children. Then they want to resort to drugs or a boot camp of some sort to do the job for them, cause they are too stupid or lazy to do the job themselves. Just look at it, Children always love their teachers that are a little bit harder on them, just a little bit more than the other teachers. Don't they? I don't mean they need militaristic discipline, but somewhere in that scope of things. And definitely not the kind of love some teachers are willing to give, but that's another story of stupid Americans for you. Love and discipline go hand in hand, John Lennon sang all you need is love. There was a man about 2000 years ago that came up with that idea. His name was Jesus. I will do my best to share my thoughts on this subject.

This nation has raised a lot of very stupid people. So there are going to be a lot of over zealous idiots out there that will go to some sort of extreme stupidity, and violence even. But I hope you can understand.

Part I: What's up with the U.S. obsession with Oprah?

Now I don't want anyone to hate me to the extent of stalking or anything like that, to any extent at all really. I'm sure she is a nice person. I just don't agree with many of her views. With that said. I suppose I should give some reasons for my discontent with said named. She gives away things on her TV show so that the whole nation will just be so amazed and impressed. What? .....Doesn't she think she is famous enough? I don't really think that it helps many of the needy people in this nation. Besides, I've always heard a real hero helps others without getting any glory or recognition for it. I've heard a lot of other talk show personalities and other celebrities who seem to have grown weary of her so called "acts of kindness." Or is it publicity hunger? But, in her defense I have seen where her production company had sent a reporter to one African nation. Where guerilla fighters would terrorize rape and murder entire villages. Getting this sort of thing seen and recognized helps in its solving. To bad we didn't have this kind of media to make the world aware. When these kinds of things were happening in Europe 700 or 800 years ago. You know she sent someone else though. She's got shows back here to do. Besides, they'll rape and kill your ass over there.

Like I said, she is a good person. She isn't the only person of wealth in this world that could use an attitude adjustment. It's the wealthy people in this nation that keep people of different nationalities. Or **<u>race</u>** as they would say, at odds with each other. **BUT** That would be stereo typing wealthy people, now wouldn't it?........ .... Shame on me.

The focus of my writings is really to look at how this nation wants to keep most of its population stupid. I'm not really sure if it is the government or just the people of the nation in general. I think maybe a combination of both. With an emphasis toward the people themselves Because, they are the ones who elect their government. "Government of the people, by the people" you know.; Along with "race" relations, and many other stupidities throughout this entire nation. Wether you are white, black, or any skin-tone between. This was as good a place to start as any.

I saw Oprah when she went to the colonial house (a show on pbs). And she talked about how hard it was for the Europeans that first came to this area that became our nation. Which was exactly correct. I thank her for that keen observation. Life has sucked for everyone for a very long time. My people being Christian, have been enslaved and tortured in some way shape or form for many years, (muchos años). Roughly 2000 of them I believe, and still are in some parts of the world.

Oprah had some show where she took jeans and other clothes and dolls to children in Africa. I couldn't stand her little speech about how every little black girl needs a black doll. {You know there are a lot of black, white, brown or any "color" of child here in this nation without dolls of their own skin tone. Or homes, and even food in their stomach, but everyone wants to go to Africa. (Winfrey, Pitt, Jolie, and a multitude of musicians. Why not help the people here in our own nation?)} Well the dolls Oprah took were probably made in china, now weren't they. You know most every little thing in your house has a little sticker on it saying made in china, Taiwan, Malaysia or some other Asian country. Where labor, verging on slave and/or child labor was used to make it. (Just because, every wealthy person around the world wants to save a penny). There is nothing that says made in Africa, or any of the countries on that continent. In any great quantities anyway. Now please don't think I harbor any Ill temper toward any Asian culture either. People are people wherever they are born. Steven Tyler says it best in song "If you can tell a wise man by the color of his skin, then mister you're a better man than I"

Just as another thought. I saw Vanessa Marcil on the Tony Danza show one morning. She was saying she was doing something with funds to build schools in Africa. She is of Mexican heritage I believe, and she seems to be doing more for the people of Africa than Oprah. What's up with that? OH yea, that's right. Every little black girl needs a black doll. Evidently that is more important than any education and a father and mother that can support a family and their household.

PART II: COMEDIANS

I saw Jamie Fox on 60 minutes one night after making the film Ray, now that is one smart man. He was talking about an earlier movie he had done. He spoke of people making jokes about themselves. As in a person of a certain ethnic group making jokes of stereo typical situations of his/her own ethnic group. I don't know. But I think, this brings that kind of situation to a forefront. People then can address their feelings and stupidities about the subject at hand. Hopefully see the humor and vulgarity. Then change to, or keep the more intelligent view. Sure, there are going to be masses of stupid people out there. No matter what Nationality you are dealing with. Stupid knows no "color or race", religion, nor any other boundaries. Nor, intelligence knows them either. Later I was watching Mr. Fox on an HBO special. I was just bursting with laughter. I had never seen any comedian talk about, and state that no race was better than any other.   And "you better blow that shit out."

Another thing that really chaps my hide. I have seen at least two black comedians in recent past state that everyone wants to be black these days. Well, In the past or even today when black people straighten and color their hair use wigs and weaves. A white person better never say that everyone seems to want to be white. That would be what this nation calls "PREJUDICE." But, There has never been a white entertainment television, an NAAWP ,or even an Ivory magazine. There use to be a lot of white only things, but that was stopped by law. Which is only the right thing to do. I mean the past is the past, why don't everyone just leave it that way and get on with it. And quit being so bigoted against any "color", religion, language, or anything else. In this country we are all americans born and raised. I had a "native American" gentleman at a Lewis and Clark exposition tell me. "Being born here makes us all native americans, doesn't it?" I thought, those are My sentiments exactly. If someone wants to refer to themselves as Asian American or African American or any other nation, place, or continent. Send them back there then. For we're all just americans here. (United States people that is)(The whole world seems to call united states people **"americans"**)(no lo se por que). Everyone wants to go home, RIGHT?

Just another thought. One Job that I worked at for a while, for a temporary agency in the midwest. I remember I worked with a number of Spanish-speaking people (Cubans', Mexicans' central americans) and a number of black and white americans. I was interested in the Spanish language which I had been learning bits and pieces since my days in the army. There was even minor tension there between speakers of english, and the ones speaking spanish. And the music each of them played. (Now ain't the people in this country Grand?)................ There was this young black man saying. "You know ebonics. You know they were teaching it in schools for a while." It just made my skin crawl. That form of speech referred to as Ebonics should have been called Ivonics, now shouldn't it have? That is if you wanted to label it at all. This was just the way that white plantation workers taught the black slaves to speak English. These workers were poor white folks that weren't extremely educated and spoke in that reprehensible manner. They taught the Spanish-speaking blacks to speak English. The N-word is just that form of word. The blacks that came from the Carribean spoke spanish. Negro is the spanish word for the color black. The spanish word for a black man is Negro and black woman is Negra. When the uneducated white plantation workers couldn't or wouldn't pronounce it like a spaniard. It came to be the N-word that black americans refer to each other so frequently. **Cause Spanish is a different language! "Duh"** The "E" doesn't sound like an E in most cases of English. In fact, I think the letter E has only one sound in the spanish language. The letter i makes the sound of the English letter E. In spanish and most other languages as a matter of fact, "I think anyway". It is the letter I that makes the eee sound. Like in the word chili, an English-speaking American has two

Part III: Who invented slavery?

This nation had a big production in the seventies over the mini series "Roots". The wealthy contingent in the nation wanted to fan the flames, of "racial" tension a bit I suppose. Well most of the blacks who came here to this area that became our nation, that came from Africa. Came via islands in the Caribbean. Not directly from Africa. I'm **not** saying that it never happened, but in general. The Portuguese and Spanish traders **bought** most black people as convicts and POW's from kings of african tribes. You see the tribal chiefs from many nations in Africa sold their convicts to the spanish and Portuguese ship owners and/or captains. They in turn brought them to the Carribean to sell as slave labor to the sugar plantation owners. I mean think about it. It is not easy to catch any thing alive. A bunch of sailors that live on a small boat out at sea for who knows how long. They aren't going to be marathon runners now are they? Hunting down Human prey, that live in the jungle and are accustomed to the habitat and any pitfalls there in. And doing all of this without harming these people enough to make a 3000 mile journey, shackled together in the hull of a ship. I think the black men would have had them rounded up, don't you? You see the African chiefs were using them as a penal institution in the same way the Brit's used the continent of Australia. It was an infinite sentence for any convict, because the chiefs had no way of retrieving them after they had payed any debt they owed to that society. Kind of like severing a hand that is of no use. That is why the Caribbean islands are predominantly black. The Spanish and Portuguese people brought so many blacks for slave labor to work their sugar plantations and what have you. Soon the blacks out numbered the whites, and revolts ensued. I've always said, "if it weren't for the Iberian Peninsula. Those black people would never have left the African continent." I mean why would anyone want to leave? It's a beautiful tropical continent. Tell me, who would want to leave? (The Iberian peninsula is the countries of Spain, Portugal, and a bit of France). I'm not saying there were never any people that were brought here directly from Africa, But not as many as the people in this nation tries to make you think. So are most black Americans, African Carribean americans? HMM.............

I suppose this nation just wants to keep its people stupid. I don't think it has been that way from the beginning. I don't know when it started really, but I don't think our founding fathers had that in mind. Although, in the movies Mel Gibson talked about trading one tyrant 3000 miles away, for 300 of the same in our front yard............ Or something like that. Kind of makes you think. Hmm...............

Many people traded and sold slaves all around the world and to the U.S. for years though, that was after someone else sold the people to them. The slave trade wasn't only black Africans. There were and still are slaves of any skin tone. There were even white slaves in this area that became our nation. Some Europeans would sell themselves and their families into slavery for the passage to the new world. They usually had a contract though, stating how long of servitude they were obligated to fulfill. But the people buying people are unscrupulous and don't adhere to contracts. Anyway that was the individuals selling themselves, not a tyrannical chief selling people as their own property.

In the same way as most Americans complain today about how Mexicans come here and take all the jobs. I'm sure there were plenty of union supporters in the north, that would complain how runaway slaves came north and took their jobs. That is why the underground railroad went all the way to Canada. Any runaway slaves caught in the north would be sent back to slavery. The hypocritical Americans thought slavery was wrong, but complained about people coming a taking their jobs. You see it seems everything goes around in a circle, like a big track for the race we're all in.

In 1712 there was a slave revolt in New York. Causing 6 blacks to commit suicide, another 21 people were executed. " Hunh!?! But that wasn't a slave state you say?" Well, they used slaves all over the americas. (Remember this wasn't even a nation at that time, that area may have still been known as New Amsterdam even). It was just hard to bring the black slaves from the Tropical Caribbean and Africa into the cold harsh winters of the north. So most of the black people were sold south to areas with more favorable climate. Then it seems once they finally became a nation the northern states got a bit anxious. That by their own doing. Their southern counterparts were getting wealthy from the virtually free labor that they couldn't use in the northern states. And, they didn't like the financial implications. So, it seems the war between the states was more over money than for any other reason. Doesn't it? HMM.... scratch your head once again. But this nation says it was the war that set America free. I'm not saying slavery was not even an issue, because it most definitely was. Slavery is a very dastardly institution, no matter what your skin color or religious background. On the other hand, an activist of today may argue the issue of embryonic stem cell research is an issue of equal prominence. And then you have the issue of same sex marriage. Now I don't really want to come off bigoted about any political issues here. A lot of people may think I sound bigoted enough the way it is. So I'll leave those issues up to you. Slavery was coming to an end in the western hemisphere at this point anyway. As early as 1777 slavery was abolished in the state of Vermont. By 1780 Gradual emancipation laws were established throughout the state of Pennsylvania. As previously stated these were northern states, and once again you have to scratch your head"HMM". In 1807 the English parliament abolished the slave trade throughout the English territories. Other countries that abolished slavery were Chile 1823, Mexico 1829, Bolivia 1831, by 1833 slavery was abolished throughout the British empire. Then many black and white americans perished in a war from 1860 to 1863, over money disputes between the United States of America. Even the southern states were freeing black slaves to fight in the war to save their money. Then at the end of that war. The 13th amendment was added to the U.S. constitution, abolishing slavery in the united states. Slavery was finally abolished in Puerto Rico in 1873, Cuba in 1880 and Brazil in 1888. I found this information on the web also. Any time slavery is mentioned though, people in this nation automatically think of the U.S. civil war. Well Slavery has been all around the world almost as long as people have been here on the world. There are still people owning other people in Africa, Russia, Mexico, India, and many other parts of the world. Probably even right here in our own great nation. Slavery wasn't invented in the United States you know, and didn't end there either. I would imagine there were people enslaved before God even made Adam......... I don't **even** want to get into that conversation. Religion is a whole other can of worms, and I could offend another genre of people.

I saw another program on pbs about the slaves Thomas Jefferson had at Monticello and his large properties. The slaves there had their own gardens that they could sell produce from. They sold fish that they caught on their own time. Jefferson even took at least one black man to France so he could learn the tin smithing trade. (That's making things out of tin, cups, plates, etc.). Sounds to me to be better than some lower middle class living of today. With housing and food furnished. I'm sure this wasn't an isolated case. Sure there were many terrible slave owners, but they couldn't have kept going for long. You couldn't stay afloat long if you are killing and maiming your workforce. Only to buy more workers to replace the ones you've maimed or killed. There always have been and still are a lot of very bad, stupid, money hungry people in the world. Slum lords and sweat shop foramen for example. People have to do a lot of things for to little money, and have to pay way to much for shoddy housing and many other things.

This nation teaches us that President Lincoln was the president who freed the black americans. In all Actuality, I read somewhere on the web that Abraham Lincoln was a colonialist. He wanted to send all the black people back to Africa. " I guess he wanted to make them colonists from the United States." I don't think that would have been such a bad deal. With ideas and their experiences from the Carribean and the united states. They may have added something to the existing culture there, and not been subjected to the bigotry, hatred, and stupidity of the reconstruction in this nation. That is still going on in places. The united states would then have colonies in Africa also. If some people didn't let any thoughts of domination take over their minds and think they had to be in complete control. Like some dictators in the Caribbean. They could have made an impact on the productivity of that continent. You never know, things might have had stickers on them today saying "made in Africa." Then, Wal-mart wouldn't have to buy **all** of their merchandise from China.

One evening I caught a program on PBS, about a black man born in1887 named Marcus Garvey. He tried to start the Black Star Line of cruise ships. He wanted to escape the hatred and bigotry here, and go with other black Americans, to start a free black nation in Africa. It seems he had the same kind of thinking and Ideas as Abraham Lincoln. FYI, the Titanic was in the white star cruise line.

I'm sorry it just seems that this country wants to keep black and white people at odds against each other. It's some, not all. But, some of the wealthy people in this nation. Not only wealthy white, but wealthy black people as well. They seem to think if they keep some animosity between blacks and whites. That it will help them make their fortunes grow. I've seen so much on pbs about this countries slavery and its hardships. Why don't they just leave it alone. That was the past. Focus on good things in the past. Besides if evolution is correct, then we all came from Africa. So I'm an African American too, My ancestors were mainly from Germany though. So they were African Germans. So I guess that would make me an African

European American. Although in this country, If your black. You are an African American, and if your white you're part of the majority. It doesn't matter where your lineage stopped off for a while between then and now. I mean there are dark people from India that idiots in this country will call african american. And then when they find out they are Indian, they will try to call them native american. You have to tell the american idiot, these people are from the country of India. Which would make them Indian Americans, when they are here in this country. Then if you have a dark native from south america, the people in this nation get really confused then. But they can't help it, this nation has taught them that way. The americans are taught that aborigines are natives of Australia. But the word aboriginal means native or original. The aboriginal people of america they call Indians, because Columbus didn't know where he was. But the aboriginal people of Australia, The american idiot will call African American, because they are black. A tan complected person coming from Egypt or Algeria, the American idiot will not call them African Anything. But that <u>is</u> northern Africa. It's just that the southern hemisphere is warmer and more directly hit by the sun. Over the centuries people there have become inherently darker. Now in more recent times people have moved all over the world. The differences of human skin tone and different cultures have moved with them. But I guess stupidity, bigotry, and hatred has come along for the ride.

Part IV: ?STUPID?

Now, what I was really wanting to focus on with this piece of writing was. How stupid do the elite classes of this nation, really want to keep the people just striving to stay alive? Of course you have to ask, how stupid does the general public here want to remain? You know, when you go to any other country. Most people there speak at least two languages, don't they? Not here in the United States. Most people in America yell "If you don't speak the language, get the fuck out of the country". But, when they travel abroad or to any other country. They show some sort of discontent. When people there in those places can't, or won't speak in English to them. Like the entire world should comply with them. I've heard the term arrogant American before, I think I can understand. Maybe the people there are thinking "If you don't speak the language, get out"! A friend I know from college told me a joke the one day. " If you have a person who speaks three languages, you call them trilingual, and a person who speaks two languages, you call them bilingual. Then what is it you call a person who speaks only one language?" Answer: an American. Now isn't that the truth? Just about any American that sees a person speaking in English and another language. The american will automatically think, " that is a smart person, they know two languages". Unless of course if it is a mexican speaking in english and spanish. Tell me why is that? Are most U.S. Americans uptight bigoted hypocrites?

Well, in the 15th and 16th centuries when the spanish conquistadors arrived. The languages of the natives of these continents must have closely mirrored or mimicked Latin languages for they seem to have picked them up quite fluently. French to the north, and spanish and Portuguese to the south. In fact the first Europeans to see the Mississippi river in the 16th century around modern day Tennessee, southern Missouri and northern Arkansas were with the Spaniard Cortez and spoke spanish. Evidently they got along well with the native inhabitants, and wintered there. (I Read that on the web too.) Lots of the names of places and sights today in this country are actually derived from (Latin) Spanish or French words, but the people in this nation aren't to intelligent. So they just say "oh that is an Indian word". And that is all over this country. More than half of the united states was Mexico before it was the United States. Or rather New Spain, Mexico didn't win its Independence until 1821. The people here spoke a creole of spanish, french, and thier native languages. Creole meaning a mixture, of the languages.

What I'm saying is, in other countries you are more likely to find people who speak in other languages other than the dominant one being spoken there. But in parts of the Americas, they may be speaking a mixture of multiple different languages. Much of south America actually speaks Portugese, although many languages could be heard in any population. Not in the united states though. Oh yes you may here other languages, but they are in very defined groups. In the united states it almost seems young people are scared to be proud of there own culture and language. Just because of the ignorant bigoted masses that will shun you for being different. Why don't people just want to be smart and learn to communicate with everyone else? Because, you know communication is the key to success in everything. And if you're a true capitalist, you can sell to a lot more people if you can speak to them in their language.

There is a very wide scope of things that American people just turn a blind eye to though. From other languages, American history, to taxes, and many other things. Hell, I don't know all of it. I was educated in the U.S. too. Like Bruce Springsteen, I was born in the U.S.A. I've just studied some of these things myself and tried to learn. That's what this wonderful country does for you. It gives you the ability and means to educate yourself. American people just have to take the initiative, and do it. I hope the powers that be don't want to stamp me out now. For anything I've said or will state in this commentary.

I know this nation doesn't like it when you talk about taxes. They sure like to recount the story of all the tea in the Boston bay though, don't they? From what I've heard, income tax was a temporary voluntary tax at its beginning. Somewhere around the WW1 era or it may have been WW2, I'm not sure. To aide in the costs of the war. And, from what I've heard it still is voluntary. But, you go to jail if you don't volunteer to pay it now. For the war, people were glad to pay at that time. But now, it is here to stay. There is no such thing as a temporary or voluntary tax in this world. You know, our government is taxing us a lot more than king George was taxing our forefathers. AND You KNOW what they did. But this nation seems a bit more capable of restraining rebels than king George's army. Rebels were taken care of in the 1860's, and no one wants to talk about the 1970's and 80's

Just the names that this country puts on things really gets my draws in a bunch. You know, look at the name "sales tax". When I'm buying something from you, you say I have to pay sales tax. I'm not selling anything! So tell me why the hell am I paying sales tax. When I see something in a store or on tv for $399.95. I end up paying more than $450.00 dollars for it. WHY! Oh I GET IT, I'm paying purchasers tax. SO WHY IN THE HELL DON'T THEY CALL IT THAT? AND INCLUDE IT IN THE PURCHASE PRICE? That is one marketing strategy it seems this

government would stop. There are so many other words that this country comes up with to. I don't think Chinese people running an ethnic restaurant in Germany refers to themselves as Asian Germans. Or a black man working in a winery in France calls himself an African Frenchman. So why is it so politically correct to use those terms in the United States. That is just a tip of the iceberg to all the other politically correct names that this nation has come up with in its stupidity.

One night I was watching the television show called "Urban Latino". There was this young man who was an artist. He stated that His mother had instilled his native American heritage in him. He was making art of his native American heritage he so loved. People in the art industry told him that there wasn't such a market for that sort of merchandise. But, he went on with his own ideas. Which I commend him for that. Then I think, what has that got to do with the urban Latino? Latin is a European word and culture isn't it? Latin is the language coming from the roman empire. And for the word Hispanic. The city of Seville in Spain was known as Hispalis to the Romans. So Hispanic people are from Europe also. But, you have all kinds of native Americans and black americans in this nation that call them selves Latino or Hispanic. Now why is that? Correct me if I'm wrong, but I think it is this nation. I don't really think that Carribean people, Mexicans, central or south Americans. Or any other culture for that matter call themselves either of those names, until they have spent time here in this nation. If that be the case, tell me. Are French speaking

Canadians Latinos also? For french is a Latin language. In the philippines there are a lot of spanish names and they speak a spanish dialect. Are they latin, hispanic or asian? HMM........ Hispasian I suppose, and when they live in this country. It would make them Hispasian American. Come on people, their just human beings in America just like you and me. **Human** is the only race being run here.

I spent some time in south Texas, And while living there. If I had a problem with athletes foot or some other chafing problem of that nature. Where I needed some Lamisil. I could go to Mexico and get some medication that would take care of the problem with a few applications. But, in this nation you can't get anything that will take care of something like that very quickly. You have to pay a doctor for a few visits and get some weak version of the medication that will finally take care of the problem after weeks of application. After you have spent all of your money, that you had to pay your bills or anything that comes up. But the doctor and drug companies can pay their bills for sure. Can't they? This nation has put regulations and limits on everything. To keep its people stupid and just healthy enough to make the rich person richer, and keep the poor ones in their place. While in San Antonio, I saw a T-shirt with this inscription. Which I found to be somewhat poetic........

Mexican
Latinos are white people from Italy
Hispanics are white people from Spain
Yo soy mexicano!
I'm a mexican!

Now, in the way this article has been going. You might accuse me of being prejudice against someone or everyone or whatever you want to think.

Oh contraire, for the word prejudice comes from the prefix pre and the word judge. Most Americans probably wouldn't even know that. I try never to prejudge anyone though. I like to communicate. Engage in intelligent conversation. Find out a persons personality, attitude, and level of intelligence. Then, and only then do I make the decision to like or dislike them. Never to hate any person. Like I've always said hate is a very strong word I don't like to use, and I never want to do. Now you may accuse me of being bigoted against stupid people. That may be the case. You see, You don't have to remain ignorant. You may have to be born to a certain family, place, or personal designation. There is nothing stopping you from educating yourself and being kind to one and other. Even a child or a person who lacks the mental capacity to grasp life. They have to be taught to hate or any form of stupidity of that kind. So please don't be the one to teach stupidity to anyone.

Part V: The Storm

In August of 2005 the United States was devastated by Hurricane Katrina. It really hurt my heart to see all the suffering people of the gulf states. Tremendous loss of life and livelihood, especially in the city of New Orleans. The intelligence of the nation was shown here in the face of tragedy. People quickly stupidly blamed the government for not responding fast enough. They started yelling that there was racial prejudices in the helping of people. I was reading the Sept. 3rd issue of the Corpus Christi Caller-times. There was an article entitled BLACKS HARDEST HIT BY HURRICANES WRATH. One paragraph of the article went like so:

> D.J. Kelly Stood on a wet New Orleans sidewalk Friday with an American flag that he plucked from a gutter and washed with "some of my precious water" Kelly, who is black, said the disaster has nothing to do with the color

of any ones skin. He then said "Don't
make it seem like no racial thing, we all
is in this together".

Now why can't everyone be as smart as this man?   No,
you have people looting, raping, and adding to the
death total.

1. I saw a PBS show about credit card fraud, and there was some lady telling how a criminal would do something. I thought about it, and it came to me. You know, there are some stupid criminals out there that wouldn't know how to do that. But they do now, if they are watching this show. Thanks to television, it's a wonderful teaching method isn't it?

2. I saw a bit of the great race one night and they were on an island off the coast of Africa. They were saying that this island was where they held slaves before taking them to the Americas. I don't really know, cause I wasn't there. And this world has lied to me so much. But that would make that island like our Alcatraz, holding prisoners there wouldn't it? They weren't slaves yet. Wether they were going to the Americas or not. Remember slavery has been all around the world for a very long time. If it weren't

for some very liberal minded people in our nation. Don't you think our government would SELL our convicts at Alcatraz to some guys on a ship that just came out of the sky? That were a different color than us, speaking in a strange language, but had something that we wanted. I'm not sure what it was those sailors gave those tribal chiefs, but it was enough to buy people.

3. The word Colony and forms of it are pretty good words people came up with. You see Christopher Columbus was an Italian. In Italy and Spain, his name is Cristobal Colon. He colonized the Caribbean islands. A museum worker in Corpus Christi TX told me it came from something meaning "do it like Colon". In latin languages, you always use the long sound of an O.

4. I just saw something about government dietary guide lines. Now what would I or anyone else want to listen to wealthy people and a government who lies about everything to them.

5. I saw Morgan Freeman on Charlie Roads show one night. There was a commercial for his narration of a pbs special on slavery. I recall him saying this nation was a slave owning nation longer than it has been a free nation. Just a minute now, there is a lot of people learning things from these pbs shows, isn't there? So why do they broadcast untruths? If this nation started in 1776, by the way they didn't have a president until 1789. The civil war was over

in 1865. Well 1776 to 1865 is just 89 years. The year 1776 to 2005 is 229 years. Lets recalculate now, 89 is about 39% of 229. Over half means, over 50%, doesn't it? But 39 % is less than 50%. I'm sorry. I don't mean any disrespect Mr. Freeman, I know it's the script writers............ I have heard a lot of ill educated americans make that same statement.

6. Talking about stupid. In this nation you have 1 out of 3 people who are over weight or obese. You see the governing of people here in this nation has made them so lazy and stupid, they don't even know when to stop eating and start walking. I knew a lady who had spent time in Italy, and she was telling me. You couldn't even drive a car in town there. She said it was for pollution control. I thought it may be because of the small roads. It could be for either or both reasons, but it definitely would help an obesity problem. Would it not?

7. I saw the CBS evening news on the night of Monday February 14th 2005. There was a gentleman that had worked on the social security project when it began, or sometime during its beginning. He said something about a $90,000 income cap. I'm not sure, but it sounded like the first $90,000 is all that they tax for social security. I mean, what it sounded like to me was a person making $90 thousand per year and a person making $4 million dollars per year is taxed the same amount for social security. So what's up with that? You know when

that rich person becomes the age to retire, he or she is going to make damn sure they get the same amount if not more of social security benefit as a person who averaged $90,000 a year. Cause a rich persons favorite thing is to get anything for free.

8. I saw Queen Latifah on David Letterman show one night, talking about her movie "beauty shop". It was showing a clip from the movie where she was yelling this statement a few times "is it because I'm black". Come on people. How long is everyone going to use that for some kind of cop out. White people as well as black have to give it up. We are all Gods chosen people. The ones of us that are homo sapiens, the human race that is.

9. I saw on the news one night about a girl that put some stuff on her legs. Then wrapped them in plastic wrap to prepare for hair removal. And on the way to the plastic surgeon she passed out in the car, and went into a coma. Ultimately she passed away from her stupidity. All this in the quest for beauty, with the least amount of work. God forbid if a doctor tells people "Drink a little bit of liquor and put this cream on your face and place a plastic bag loosely over your head before you go to sleep, it will make you look younger." Now that would thin out a lot of the stupid ones wouldn't it? (I saw a comedian one time talk about people thinning the herd, like gazelles)

10. Then you have a thirty two year old woman who runs off and makes a 911 call and tells officials that she has been kidnaped so she can skip out on her wedding. Then the media plays it up so much and glamorizes the act, so all the other americans have one more obstacle to overcome when they are trying to teach their own children how to act. But, what kind of nation educated a woman like that? And then she makes a lot of money for her story. It just don't figure, does it?

11. You know they have assassinations in other parts of the world, But they are mostly politically motivated. Aren't they? What exactly was John Lennon shot for in this country. (Was it because this nation loves stupid people?) ? HMMM........... .... It must, they give $millions$ to a woman that burns her coochie with some hot coffee....... Now you can't even get a good cup of coffee at McDonalds.

12. They even let idiots in this nation put things on the internet. That's technology for you. There was a sight I found about Maximilian. He was an Austrian that the french appointed as Emperor of Mexico in the 1800s. It was supposed to be a funny site I suppose. But the idiot said Maximilian didn't speak spanish or french. It was the idiot that made the sight that couldn't understand anything he read. Maximilian was of the Hapsburg Dynasty (the ruling family of the Austro-Hungarian empire). He and his wife had a castle built for them in Trieste

Italy, near Slovenia. They called it Miramar castle because it overlooks the Adriatic sea. Miramar means Look at the sea in Italian and spanish, those two languages are almost Identical. He probably spoke french too.

13. In this nation People think we invented slavery, and the wheel too I suppose. In the movies you never see any of the native americans pulling a wagon, cart, or anything with wheels. How do you think the natives got the corn, squash, and beans that they grew from place to place. They may not have had horses until the spanish brought them here. I'm sure they had to transport their grain and other crops in some way though. The Incan natives in south America had hundreds of miles of roads DUH!?! Ya think they may have had a cart to pull?

14. Oh, my favorite, Oprah. I just saw where she had a party at her "California estate" for black women of achievement. Why is it deemed prejudice if a person would have something to commemorate the accomplishments of white people? But, you can do anything you want for black people. There is never anything said about any other people, only blacks. What? No other people have ever accomplished anything? I wonder if there are things in any other countries to commemorate the accomplishments of any certain people, religion, or any other specific "race". HMMM...

15. Talk about stupid, When anything of any importance is done. A person in the U.S. will say "only in america". Well Adolph Hitler was a Corporal in the Austrian army in WW1. And, in 18 years or less, he was the leader of a world power (Germany). He was a crazed maniac, that wasn't in america. Joseph Stalin was born in Georgia (a small country between Turkey and Russia) and he rose to a very powerful position. Both Hitler and Stalin in countries different from their birth. Karl Marx was born in Germany, and was exiled to France and Great Britain. When anyone mentions Marx in America, people will automatically think of Russia. Because of his Communist Manifesto, that he wrote while living in Germany. You see europeans are inevitably required to learn more than one language.

16. I think the entire world calls it the Mediterranean sea. I think that this pronunciation came from speakers of english. You see, the roman word for sea was and is mare. To an english speaking person. When an italian says that word. It sounds more like mahrday. The romans would say the subject first, so the word sea would come first. Then the name of the sea, which they called Internum (meaning inside). So they said mare internum. Which would sound like Mahrday eentearnum. {This meaning the sea inside} for romans thought it was the center of the earth. When english speaking people heard the words (mare internum) they must have

thought this was one word. Thats how it became Mediterranean. The romans also called it Mare Nostrum. Which means our sea,. You see the roman empire encompassed the Mediterranean. (Went all the way around it that is.)

17. I've heard so much about the moors in Spain and the Moorish influences in Mexico. I don't know, is that a word that this country came up with? Do they teach that word in other countries? Where exactly did the moors come from? Moorland or Moorville? I understand there was a conquering culture of Islamic people that took over Spain for a time. And there are Islamic masques in Spain. As a matter of Fact, I visited Mission San Jose in San Antonio Texas. There, I saw a mechanical water wheel that was turning counter clockwise. The guide was telling everyone that it was because of the Moorish influence from Spain. Because the moors were from the southern hemisphere. I thought about it, and it came to me. These so called Moors couldn't have come from the southern hemisphere. That is the southern third of the African continent. I read there were a lot of people from the country of Yemen in the town of Seville. But that is the southern part of the Arabian peninsula, which is in the northern Hemisphere. I don't know It just amazes me, the stranglehold grip that stupidity has on this entire nation.   { FYI, and for my information too. I have found that it was the Italians that called them the moors. Because they

were from the country of Mauritania in north Africa. (by the way, Mauritania is in the northern hemisphere)}

18. I hear so many people complain about The ATM asking if you want your transaction in english or spanish. And they complain about everything comes with instructions in so many different languages. People in this nation will scream "your in America, learn to read english". Well people, the town of Nice in france is close to Monaco and the Italian border. The street signs there are in two languages. In Quebec (Canada) all the signs and store fronts are in two languages. They don't have a national language in Austria or Switzerland. Before WW1 they were part the Austro-Hungarian empire and at least 15 languages were spoken in that empire. That was in an area no larger than three or four states in the midwest. Like I said, just be kind to one another. If nothing else body language and hand motions is a universal language. My mother use to tell me a rhyme "when its hot he wants it cold, and when its cold he wants it hot, always wanting what is not" that's just the way americans are I guess. People all around the world are that way though, I think.

19. What's up with this country? I saw on TV one night that they are passing laws that cities and counties can take peoples land and property, if they think it will be a benefit to the local economy. You know people can go on television and win houses

and prizes or even a million dollars for doing really stupid things. What is this world coming to?

20. I saw the movie "In My Country". And the part where Samuel Jackson (Quoted in the movie: " an african american")was talking to Juliette Binoche, a white woman born in south africa. She said she was an african, which was exactly correct. Samuels character says "not in my book". That just shows you the vastness of the stupidity taught in this nation. (Again: I'm not meaning any disrespect to Mr. Jackson, He is a great actor) But that is like Cheech Marin's song, Born in east L.A. Which makes him an American. It all comes down to where you were born, Right? Now there are americans in the military, and if their children are born in other countries that is a different story. Their parents are U.S. citizens so it makes them americans. That goes for any countries Military.

21. On the night of July 22nd 2005 there was an article on 60 minutes where these two kids beet this other child to death. And wether they could try them as adults or not. They killed him because he was a little different. Mentally challenged or something like that. They were interviewing the kids, and one of them seemed a little challenged himself. The interviewer had to explain numerous words to him, Is that the intelligence of an average 13 year old american? The other one just seemed mean. But this is the kind of children this nation is producing.

22. On the same night of July 22nd, 48 hrs had a report on enslaved women traded in Russia and Mexico. Who started this thing slavery? OH YEA it was people wasn't it? So you can hold everyone responsible

23. On July 26th , '05 I saw an episode of wide angle on pbs. Bill Moyers was interviewing a very intelligent man named George Ayittey. Ayittey a Native of Ghana, and noted economist and professor at an American University in Washington DC. Ayittey spoke of the corrupt governments in many of the African nations and how they needed some tough love, not just throwing money at them. Bill Moyers spoke about how The american politicians were afraid to speak out about black african leaders, for fear of being labeled as racists. Which is exactly true. The american public has been made so stupid that there would be a major backlash across the nation. Ayittey was saying how the African governments need to be corrected from within. In other words, work on and fix their corruption themselves. It seems to me that the whole world just keeps giving them money, while their corrupt government ("the elite class" as Ayittey puts it) squanders any and all help given to them. I mean, look at it. The elite classes were selling human beings to any sailors that happened to come by for years.

24. Now in this country the elite classes run the show also. Only on a bit of a different scale. If the American public doesn't screw their head back

on tight, and start educating themselves. Who knows what could happen in this nation. Like I said, this is the greatest nation in this world. It gives everyone the chance and ability to educate themselves. America just has to do it. Like Nike says "just do it"

25. I saw Bill Mahr on the David Letterman show in August of 2005. He was talking about television shows in the sixties, and the different content in shows of today. He was saying how the american public is stupid these days. So I guess I'm not the only one thinking that way. Myself I think the dumbing of america has been going on for a very long time though. It just seems to have taken a drastic decline in the past fifty years or so.

26. Now the title of this being about the evils of money. You know, you can kill someone in this country and get away with it. But, if you do anything wrong with money. You'll go to jail. Just look at Martha Stuart.

27. I caught a PBS episode on Thursday Aug. 25th 2005. Once again the NCAA was crying about Chief Iliniwik at Illinios University. I think they should just change the name of the state, that goes for any state or anything named with native names in this nation. Then maybe people will stop crying about disgracing anyone. Most of the native languages were just wiped out and forgotten from these continents anyway. You think maybe when

everything related to natives is gone in this nation, that will make the american idiots shut up?

Now, don't get me right. I think this nation is the best in the world, people in it just need to get a clue. That is why everyone wants to come to **"america"**. The united states that is. I love you all, I thank you for letting me vent my opinions. Just think about it............ and try to learn something good. And Please be kind to one and other.

This is one American
just happy to be alive
gracious a Dios
That's (thanks to god)in spanish
Spain: A European country, its just the language spoken
south of the border,

Oyvin DeScoyvin

Post script

Back on the subject of skin tone. Black and white are not even colors. They aren't in the rainbow, are they? You can put them into colors to change the tint of that color. Anyway, People of the tropics and the southern hemisphere have become inherently darker in skin tone. Although, People of Egypt, Libya, Algeria, and all of north Africa. They are not black Africans, so an American idiot would not call those people african anything. People of Europe refer to those people as Mediterranean types. Being darker in complexion with darker hair and eyes. When the Roman empire stretched around that sea, skin tones evened out. A person from Tunisia, Algeria, or Libya, which is Africa. Have the same complexion or close to it, as a person from Sicily or southern Italy which is Europe. In Germany you may hear whiter blond men refer to a darker lady as, "a left over roman." You see the farther north you go. People have become lighter in skin tone, the less time they and their ancestors have spent in the sun. Where as people on the southern side of the world and their ancestors have spent more time exposed to the sun. They have grown inherently darker, and passed it on to their offspring and down through the ages.

Come to think about it... We use the roman alphabet don't we? So how much does it really take to be Latin? Africa is the cradle of life, and we use the roman alphabet. So I guess that would make me an African Latin German American. But Africa is a continent, Latin is a culture, and Germany is a country. So what exactly is the basis of these "race" categories. Oh well, I guess we all have to live in this world.

Adios Muchachos Y Muchachas

ABOUT THE AUTHOR

Oyvin Descoyvin was born Harold Hughes in a small community in northwest Missouri. Then in infancy moved with his family to a suburb of Kansas City MO. At age eight he and his family moved to a rural farm close to a town of 999 population. This is where little Harold grew up and graduated. After completing elementary, Junior high, and High school all in the same building. Harold went on to serve honorably in the US army. While in school he wasn't a studious child, you could say somewhat slacking in his studies. He did just enough to squeak by with passing grades. They probably would have diagnosed him with something in to days' society. He was just a little lazy and rebellious. They did put him in some slow learning remedial classes. Anyway, he graduated on time. Then it was off to the United States army. This is where Oyvin was created. You see, at birth Harold's mother gave him the middle name of Irwin. There was a typing error on the certificate and the w became a v. When Harold joined the army, his drivers license had his middle name as Irvin. The specialist in the arms room of 1/69 armor, (this was the unit Harold was sent to in Germany) pronounced the name "Oyvin". Harold became good friends with the soldier and DeScoyvin soon followed the name Oyvin. Harold/Oyvin completed his four year enlistment, and received an honorable discharge. Harold/Oyvin started college shortly after leaving the army, and was well on his way. Unfortunately three quarters of the way to his graduation, Harold had an auto accident. The accident left him in a coma for 31 days. His family was not given very much hope. But with the grace of god the father and Jesus Christ, Harold pulled through and spent a total of nine and a half months in the hospital. He had to endure many trials and tribulations after being discharged from the hospital working many late nights and long hours. Finally returning to college to finish the degree he had started. Whilst in college for the second time, he was talking to a professor that he had learned from prior to the accident. Her words were quite inspirational; she said, "Harold, many people that went through a traumatic accident like that, would not go on to finish what they had started". My reply was "I hope a prospective employer will think that one day". It hasn't happened yet. Harold has had to face many trials and tribulations and ridicule even, during all the turmoil he has endured. The Oyvin persona wanted to record some music to accompany this book. We will have to see how well it is received, and maybe. Just maybe the music could follow.